BACK-TO-SCHOOL FRIGHT
FROM THE
BLACK LAGOON

BACK-TO-SCHOOL FRIGHT
FROM THE
BLACK LAGOON

by Mike Thaler
Illustrated by Jared Lee
SCHOLASTIC INC.

New York Toronto London Auckland Sydney
Mexico City New Delhi Hong Kong Buenos Aires

To
Gary & Chris Stubbs,
Hearts always open
—M.T.

To Roger and Jenny Schinbeckler
—J.L.

ISBN-13: 978-0-545-07221-2
ISBN-10: 0-545-07221-2

Text copyright © 2008 by Mike Thaler
Illustrations copyright © 2008 by Jared D. Lee Studio, Inc.

All rights reserved. Published by Scholastic Inc.

SCHOLASTIC, LITTLE APPLE, and associated logos are trademarks and/or registered trademarks of Scholastic Inc.

Lexile is a registered trademark of MetaMetrics, Inc.

12 11 10 9 8 7 6 5 4 3 2 1   8 9 10 11 12 13/0
Printed in the U.S.A.
First printing, September 2008

CONTENTS

BLAST OFF!

WOW!

ELM LEAF

CHAPTER 1
THE FALL OF MAN

DRAT.

The leaves are beginning to fall, and so are my spirits. I guess that's why they call it the "fall." Each leaf that hits the ground is a nail in the coffin of summer.

MAPLE
← LEAF

BUG

What can I do to extend the vacation? I could put a "For Sale" sign in front of the school. I could change the street signs so nobody can find it. I could change everybody's calendar. I could glue all the leaves back on the trees—*sigh*. . . . I think it'll just be easier to go back to school.

BLACK LAGOON ELEMENTARY

FOR SALE

$1.00

CHAPTER 2

AM I BLUE?

My fate is sealed. All the stores know it. They're all having back-to-school sales. Hey, if they're so excited about it, why don't *they* go back to school, and let us kids work in the stores.

Mom says we have to go shopping. I know what that means. I go, but she picks out all my clothes. And we don't have the same taste at all.

I'll want the new Slime Monster shirt that will make everyone holler. And she'll pick a baby-blue shirt with a tiny, "cute" collar. But her vote seems to rate higher than mine. So I will be blue for sure.

11

CHAPTER 3
MALLED AGAIN

The mall is crowded. It's full of mothers dragging around unhappy kids. It doesn't feel like shopping to me—it feels more like chopping.

Mom says I need new shirts, shoes, pants, and underwear. There's nothing wrong with my underwear, and my pants have just gotten comfortable. It's taken me a year to break them in. Moms don't understand the concept—'cause just when they're perfect, they throw them away.

CHAPTER 4
A SHOE-IN

Our first stop is the shoe store. It's called The Athlete's Toes. Wow, there's a brand-new pair of Superstar Rainbow High Jumper Glow-in-the-Dark Slam Dunk Stratofearless Rocket-Assisted

Space Walkers—and they're only $255. Mom leads me over to a nice, durable pair of brown, all-purpose dress shoes. A real square pair.

17

I run back to the Superstar Rainbow High Jumpers and hold them to my chest. It doesn't work. The salesman brings out a boring pair of brown clods and puts them on my feet. They don't bounce, they don't spring, they don't light up, they don't sing. Why is it that salesmen always stick together with moms? It's a conspiracy. I guess they know moms have the money. And money speaks louder than tears. It's the holler of the dollar, the bash of the cash, the honey of the money.

BEEP!

BEEP!

18

CHAPTER 5
GLOW FOR IT

Well, the rest of the shopping trip doesn't go much better. I've got a nice blue shirt with a little collar and brand-new pants so stiff that I can't bend at the knees.

CUTE TINY, LITTLE COLLAR →

BABY BLUE →

WILL NOT BEND →

STIFF AS A BOARD

I did have a minor victory, though. I got to choose a pair of fluorescent, glow-in-the-dark underwear. Of course, no one will ever see it, but I will know.

* "ROGER THAT" IS ARMY TALK FOR "I UNDERSTAND."

CHAPTER 6
MEASURING UP

Next we buy school supplies. Mom rejects a whoopee cushion and plastic vomit. But we do get notebooks, pencils, erasers, and a ruler. Whoopee! This semester is going to be a blast. I'll get a new pencil sharpener. Maybe it'll make me sharper in class.

PIG BOY →

CHAPTER 7
PANT-O-MIME

When we get home, Mom takes my old pants and goes to throw them out before I can hide them.

JOCKEY →

I'm trying to save them when Eric calls.

He's back from baseball camp and has lots of stories. He says we'll touch base later; now he has to go shopping with *his* mom . . . good luck!

· THINGS YOU LEARN AT ·
BASEBALL CAMP

① HOW TO BAT   ② HOW TO PITCH

③ HOW TO CATCH

④ HOW TO STEAL

⑤ HOW TO SLIDE   ⑥ HOW TO THROW

←PITCHER   27

SPIDER → ← SNACK

CHAPTER 8
FOOD FOR THOUGHT

Freddy calls. He's home from chef camp. It was called "Wieners for Winners." He tells me he learned 200 ways to cook hot dogs. He made: hot dog fricassee; soufflé of hot dog; hot dog Stroganoff; hot dog Parmesan; macaroni and hot dogs; hot dog tacos; hot dog pizza; and hot dogs Benedict.

BUN

MUSTARD

HOT DOG

BUN

I ask him what he's having for dinner tonight—he says, "hot dogs." I ask him why he's not out shopping with his mom. He says she goes shopping by herself and leaves him at home. Somehow that's a lot more reasonable.

31

CHAPTER 9
OUTFITS TO BE TIED

HI, HUBIE.

NOT REAL ↓

SAY, "HELLO" FOR ME.

FRIENDLY ↗ BIRD

Next Doris calls. She says her mom bought her beautiful new dresses. She just loves them! Are girls more in tune with their moms than we are? She says she got new unicorn notebooks, princess pencils, and pink heart erasers. Sometimes I think girls have it easier than boys.

ARF! ARF!

BARKING ⟶ WORM

32

TINY CAR AND DRIVER EXACT SIZE ⟶

WHAT DORIS BOUGHT AT THE MALL

DRESSES

SHOES

SOCKS

NOTEBOOKS

PENCILS

ERASERS

RULER

33

CHAPTER 10
NEW ROOM AND GLOOM

Next Derek calls and we put together a forecast for next semester. It looks cloudy and gloomy. He says there will be more tests, more homework, more headaches, and more

IT'S NOT GOOD.

REALLY!

34

heartaches. The work gets harder and the teachers don't get any softer. There are rumors about a new one, Miss Cranky, who's so tough that the kids in her class have to take out insurance.

The perks are nonexistent. We have to eat in the same cafeteria, and the school hours don't get any shorter. Because you're older, more is expected of you. I'm worried because I think I'm operating at my max right now. I peaked in the second grade.

TODAY'S MENU
MUSH MUSH AND MORE MUSH

FREE KITTENS SEE MIKE

GADS!

↑ BONE

37

CHAPTER 11
A SCREAM DREAM

That night I have a schoolmare. I'm walking down a long hall. I'm the only one in school. All of a sudden the bell rings, and a bunch of crazed teachers rush out. They grab my arms and legs and start pulling me into their classrooms. Math goes one way, English another. History and Science yet another.

← STRESS BUG

I'm coming apart. I wasn't built for all this stress. I miss the calm of kindergarten. Back then I had it locked with blocks.

• ←— CAVITY   • ←— BLACK DOT

CHAPTER 12
A DENTURE ADVENTURE

And to make things perfect, the next day Mom takes me to the dentist. Dr. Molar is always a treat. He fills my mouth up with cotton and odd instruments. Then he asks me if I'm excited about starting school.

A SORE TOOTH ——→

After the dentist, Mom takes me to the doctor for my back-to-school shots. I wish there was a vaccination for fear.

44

CHAPTER 13
READY TO ROLL

PROUD MOM →

HUBIE, NOW YOU'RE ALL SET FOR SCHOOL.

THANKS, MOM.

I'm back in shape now from top to bottom. I have clean teeth, no major diseases, new school supplies, and clean clothes—they're not sharp, but my pencil is.

← FROGS DON'T GO TO SCHOOL

← BIRDS DON'T GO TO SCHOOL

I've been practicing getting up early and running to the bus stop. I've also been stretching. I'm a little worried that the girls have grown taller than me.

HOUSE

ROUTE →

BUS
STOP

STRETCHING CHART

Here comes the school bus. The door opens and I climb aboard.

GIANT BED BUG
(USUALLY FOUND IN A KING-SIZE BED.) →

I'M HUNGRY.

MINI BUS ↓

← SCHOOL BUS

GIANT BED BUG'S
FAVORITE SNACK ⟶

Nobody looks any happier than I feel, except maybe T-Rex, who has a big grin on his face. I wonder what he did this summer. I hope he took driving lessons.

SUPER LONG
SCHOOL BUS
⟵

51

Uh-oh, it's just as I feared.

I sit down next to Eric. "Did you notice the girls?"

"Yeah, they're taller than us."

53

"So tell me about camp."

"Well," he says, "I was a big hit at baseball camp. On the second day, I made a home run."

"You mean you hit a home run?"

"No, I mean I got homesick and ran home."

"What did your parents do?"

"Well, they said that they needed a vacation and sent me back."

"What did you do?"
"I became an umpire."

"A vampire?"

"No, an umpire. Then I didn't have to run, exercise, or sweat. All I had to do was say 'strike' or 'ball.'"

"That sounds safe."

"Oh, I had to say that, too."

57

Just then we pull up in front of the school and T-Rex does a wheelie.

"Any last words of wisdom?" I ask.

"Well," says Eric, scratching his baseball cap, "if we go on *strike*, we can have a *ball*."

CHAPTER 14
YEARN TO LEARN

Well, we didn't go on strike and we didn't get Miss Cranky. We got Mrs. Green again. She was glad to see us, and we were glad to see her.

61

She told us all the exciting new things we were going to learn about—stars and cars and faraway places. We will climb the highest mountains and explore the deepest seas. We will learn about all the animals, birds, bugs, and trees. We will be taller and smarter than ever before... 'cause the more you know—the more you grow.

Hey, let's get started. I need to catch up with the girls.